When I Was There

1

VANCOUVER 2199
BOSTON 1359
SEATTLE 210
NEW YORK 1169
MIAMI
LA 1672 mil
TORONTO 1112
HONOLULU 4213
CHICAGO

Text © 2013 Joe Van Snellenberg
Illustrations © 2013 Anna Shukeylo
Design © 2013 Inkflight Publishing

ink/light

Inkflight Publishing
Mailing address
PO BOX 4608
Main Station Terminal
349 West Georgia Street
Vancouver, BC
Canada, V6B 4A1

www.inkflight.com

Edited by: A.R. Roumanis
Illustrated by: Anna Shukeylo
Designed by: A.R. Roumanis

FIRST EDITION / FIRST PRINTING

LIBRARY AND ARCHIVES CANADA CATALOGUING IN PUBLICATION

Van Snellenberg, Joe, 1953-, author
    When I was there / by Joe Van Snellenberg ; illustrated by Anna Shukeylo.

ISBN 978-1-926606-98-9 (pbk.)

I. Shukeylo, Anna, 1988-, illustrator
II. Title.

PS8643.A597W54 2013   JC813'.6   C2013-906602-0

When I Was There

By Joe Van Snellenberg

ILLUSTRATED BY ANNA SHUKEYLO

inkflight / VANCOUVER

3

4

RUFF & MRROW LANGUAGE TRAINING

When I was in Vancouver
it was raining cats and dogs.
They landed in the streets
and floated down on logs.

They quickly whisked down Main,
then hopped on to the ground
and caught the bus at Station
that took them right downtown.

They opened up a business
a block from Stanley Park
and taught a thousand people
how to meow and bark!

WELCOME

5

When I was in Chicago
I got in trouble deep.
I drove a car the wrong way
down a one-way street.

They threw me in the jailhouse
and there upon the wall,
the skeeters and the bedbugs
played a game of ball.

The score was three to nothing,
the bedbugs were ahead,
but the skeeters hit a grand slam
and knocked me out of bed!

6

GO BUGS!

GO SKEETS

GO SKEETS

GO BUGS!

When I was in Hawaii
a volcano blew its top.
Ten people ran for cover
into a doughnut shop.

We shut the doors and windows
without much time to spare.
The lava flowed like syrup
and ashes filled the air.

We lived for two full days
on muffins and on rolls.
The third day we had doughnuts,
on the fourth we ate the holes!

When I was in Los Angeles
there was a cartoon house,
where cats played hide and seek
with an animated mouse.

The forks and knives were jamming
on the kitchen counter stage,
and a teaspoon sang out recipes
from every cookbook page.

The mop and broom boogied
with dolls, toy trucks and cars,
and I made my way to Hollywood
by dancing with the stars!

When I was in Seattle
I climbed into a boat
and set to sail the ocean
but the darn thing wouldn't float.

It creaked and reeked and like my
sneakers leaked
and the boat was going to sink.
But a seagull that was flying by
dropped something silver in my drink.

I sailed the seas for seven days,
a week I stayed afloat.
That something was a duct tape roll
that fixed the leaky boat!

When I was in Calgary
I went to the Stampede,
rode in with the cowboys
and out with tumbleweeds.

I watched the stagecoach race
and bucking broncos too,
and danced until the finals
of the western Hullabaloo.

The best darn rider there,
yes the best in the all the world,
was no wild west cowboy –
it was a Blackfoot girl!

When I was in New York, New York
I went down to Times Square,
then walked my way to Wall Street
amongst the bulls and bears.

I took the train to Central Park,
the frisbee folks were flying.
There were artists and musicians
and the crowd was multiplying.

I went to watch the Yankees play
and got to meet the Mets.
I looked up at the Giants
then flew home with the Jets!

When I was in Boston
I found a lobster claw,
but when I left the beach
I had a run-in with the law.

They thought the claw was stolen
from the Squiggly Wiggly store.
They asked a thousand questions
'til they couldn't think of more.

Finally they believed me,
there should have been no doubt,
because at Squiggly Wiggly
the lobsters were sold out!

When I was in Toronto
I took a downtown tour
from here and there to there and here,
to Yonge Street and to Bloor.

The cars honked a new language,
a Euro-Asian-Afri-tongue,
and I took some multi-culti pix
where Bloor Street meets with Yonge.

I went to Thorncliffe Park
and bowled with rich and poor.
Then struck out down the alleys
back to Yonge Street and to Bloor!

When I was in Miami
I couldn't take the Heat,
so chilled out watching Dolphins
swim and chirp and tweet.

I got some South Beach sun,
tanned my hide real well,
gathered up my surfboard
and rode the ocean swell.

I donned the snorkeling gear
and paddled with the fish,
took a break for dinner
and had a Marlin dish!

When I was in New Orleans
I swam in Bayou Bay,
where all the little fishies
made up games to play.

They sent me on an errand
down to Danger Swamp,
where crocodiles and 'gators
were waiting there to chomp.

A 'gator caught me in his teeth,
I couldn't last for long.
He opened wide so I jumped out
as he sang this song:

25

Wwwwwwhen.... I was in New Orleans
I swam in Bayou Bay,
where all the little fishies
made up games to play.

They sent me on an errand
down to Danger Swamp,
where crocodiles and 'gators
were waiting there to chomp.

A 'gator caught me in his teeth,
I couldn't last for long.
He opened wide so I jumped out
as he sang this song!

Now you've heard my stories,
you know I've been around.
Where's the place *you* want to go -
which city or which town?

Make the world your playground
and adventure will abound.
In person or imagination,
go see what can be found!

CPSIA information can be obtained
at www.ICGtesting.com
Printed in the USA
BVIC01n0309201213
339670BV00002B/3

9781926606989